Beti Rozen

A Heart Alone in the Land of DARKNESS

ILLUSTRATED BY GRAÇA LIMA

EDITED BY PETER HAYS

SEM FRONTEIRAS PRESS
FORT LEE, NEW JERSEY

Printed in China
Set in Brazil

Second edition 2004

Publisher's Cataloging-in-Publication
(Provided by Quality Books, Inc.)

Rozen, Beti.
A heart alone in the land of darkness / by Beti Rozen;
illustrated by Graça Lima ; edited by Peter Hays.--2nd ed.
p. cm.
SUMMARY: In a land where most .have forgotten their humanity a lonely heart
searches for one person who is still compassionate and open.
   LCCN 2003102088
   ISBN 0-9642333-2-0
      1. Heart--Juvenile fiction. 2. Compassion--Juvenile fiction. 3. Spiritual
   life--Juvenile fiction. [1. Heart--fiction. 2. Compassion--Fiction. 3. Spiritual-
   ity--Fiction.] I. Lima, Graca. II. Hays, Peter. III.

PZ7.R823He 2004   [E]
                    QBI33-1203

For information address:
Sem Fronteiras Press
1530 Palisade Avenue, Suite 2F
Fort Lee, NJ 07024
U.S.A.
Tel: (201) 461-1617 / Fax: (201) 461-1621
e-mail: semfront@superlink.net

A HEART ALONE IN THE LAND OF DARKNESS

by
Beti Rozen

Edited by
Peter Hays

This book is dedicated to the memory of my father,

Moszek Lejzor (Luiz) Rozencwajg.

He let a heart into his chest and never knew the
Land of Darkness.

— B.R.

In the Land of Darkness, nobody had a heart. Everyone had forgotten what it was like to be human. Days were as dark as nights because people thought with their heads instead of feeling with their hearts.

But there was a sole heart, without a home. His dream was to live inside the chest of a person so that he could become a real human being.

On a typical dark day, the Heart saw a man with a calculator. He was adding, subtracting and sometimes dividing. But his passion was to multiply, especially MONEY.

"Would you like to be my owner?" asked the Heart. "Can I enter into your chest?"

"Hearts don't talk!" snapped the impatient man. "Besides, no one here has a heart."

The red Heart was so sad that he began to pale; he became the color of a pumpkin.

"I know the language of feeling," said the Heart.

"But you understand the language of reason. You don't feel."

"Of course not!" said the man with the calculator. "My business is thinking. I must multiply; I must make money. Who cares about feelings?"

"Have you ever loved someone?" asked the Heart. "Only with a heart is it possible to love. Loving is when you care about others and wish them well. Sometimes you worry more about them than you do about yourself."

"Me? Worry about others?" said the man as he tapped on his calculator. Then he mumbled, "Must earn money, must buy, must accumulate more and more."

Do you always need more and more money for yourself?" wondered the Heart out loud. "Why can't you share? Many people don't have enough money."

"Share? Me? Share? Why do they need money? I need it. Let people work," he insisted. "You're making my head hurt. Good-bye."

The Heart followed the man. "Can I enter into your chest?" he asked one last time. "You might change and become a better person."

"I'm perfect as I am," snarled the man as he walked away. "Good-bye!" The Heart was left alone.

Later, the Heart noticed a Poet who was sitting on a park bench.

"What are you doing?" asked the Heart.

"Trying to write a poem for the girl I like," he replied.

"But how do I express my feelings?"

The Heart suddenly became excited. "Feelings? I have lots of feelings! Let me enter into your chest," the Heart suggested. "Then you can write the best love poem ever."

"Love? Stay away," said the Poet. "I suffer too much when you are around."

The Heart was shocked. "Suffer? Why?"

"Because a heart makes you feel too much," the Poet explained. "Sometimes, we expect more than people are able to give."

"But how can you write a good poem without feelings?!" exclaimed the Heart. "You need a heart!"

   "You're right," the Poet admitted. "But I'm afraid.
No one is interested in poetry nowadays. It's like talk-
ing to a brick wall."

   "Let me enter into your chest," pleaded the Heart.
"Then you can write great poetry."

   "Okay," said the Poet. "I'll give you another
chance."

   The Heart slowly entered into the chest of the Poet.

"How wonderful! How warm!" the Heart sighed.
"It's so nice to have a place to live."

For a short time, they made a perfect match.
And the Poet's love poem turned out to be his best

When the girl came along, the young writer was
so excited that he read his creation to her. But she
just stared and said, "Too many dumb feelings," and
walked away.

Upset and lovesick, the Poet wanted to tear the Heart from his chest. But it felt so warm and comfortable, the Heart hated to leave. Poor Heart, poor Poet.

The Poet made a deal with the Heart: "You can stay and help me write poems, but you must control yourself. I don't want her or anyone else to hurt my feelings again. Ever."

"It's a deal," the Heart agreed, with a sigh.

The Poet wrote another poem; it did not have much love or feeling. The Heart started to feel sick. Day and night, he was forced to control himself.

When the girl finally came back, she thought the Poet's new poem was wonderful. He, too, seemed less silly to her now, so she began to pay more attention to him.

But the Heart was miserable; he could feel the Poet pushing him out of his body. Finally, needing more freedom to feel, the tiny red Heart jumped from the Poet's chest.

The Poet felt better without the Heart. After all, he did not suffer so much because he loved less.

Without a home, the Heart was free but unhappy.

A few hours went by. The lonely Heart ran across the leader of the Land of Darkness, a man with a big mustache. He was a dictator who ordered his people around: he told them what to do, what to wear, what to eat, while he got to do whatever he wanted.

The Heart was afraid. "How can a bad person allow a heart into his chest?" he thought to himself. "This will be a challenge, but . . ."

The nervous Heart approached the Dictator. "Would you let me slowly enter into your chest?" he asked.

"What for?" barked the mean leader. "I am too busy to bother myself with a lowly heart."

"Lowly heart? I may be little," the Heart admitted "but I contain lots of love, dreams and emotions. Do you know what it is to love?"

"I love my people," said the proud Dictator who lied. "I do everything for them. Why, I even let them breathe."

"Breathing is a god given right," responded the Heart. "You don't have control over it."

"Oh really?" replied the powerful leader. "Pretty soon, I will own the air, too." Then he looked at the Heart: "It's not my fault there is not enough food to eat or clothes to wear. I cannot create miracles."

"Miracles only happen with love," the Heart pointed out. "You don't love your people. You don't care if they have enough food to eat or clothes to wear. You fight wars and let many people die. This is not love."

"Who are you to talk to me like that?" the Dictator bellowed.

"See? You want to start another war right now," the Heart continued. "This is how you love your people?" The Dictator thought it over for a moment.

"Let me inside your chest," the Heart begged.

"I will show you how to make people happier. You'll become a better person."

"I am a wonderful person!" screamed the Dictator.
Refusing to leave, the Heart stood firm: "Let's try a little
bit. We can bring light and color back into this land."

The grumpy Dictator finally gave in a little. "Considering how you pester so, I guess we could give it a try," he growled.

The Heart entered quickly into the Dictator's chest. Slowly, the leader began to change. He gave fewer orders.

Then he felt an urge to give out food to those who did not have enough to eat. It wasn't easy for the powerful leader to share—not without getting something in return—but he tried.

Feeling strange inside the mighty leader's chest, the Heart became tougher. The Dictator struggled more and more with his new heart; both of them were going against their nature.

Finally, the Dictator refused to give out any more food to hungry people. He demanded that everyone pay, even if they did not have enough money.

Next, the Dictator felt the urge to start another war. With the Heart inside his chest, he tried to stop himself, but the urge to fight was too strong.

Frustrated, the little Heart left the Dictator's chest. Once again, the Heart noticed that his red color had already begun to pale; he resembled the color of a pumpkin. Meanwhile, the Dictator was shouting, "I am the leader, commander, agitator! I have all the power! I am a friend! I want to love, but, but, but. . . nobody can breathe. Oh, I love to frighten people and tell them what to do!" He was obviously very confused.

Alone again, the Heart felt lost and sad.

Standing in the street, the Heart was quickly discovered by a woman. She appeared a lot on television and was looking for a new story.

"A heart all alone! Without a home!" she said, pretending to care. "Amazing! I'll have you on my show. Everyone will be glued to the TV. People will go crazy over you. We will have a revolution in the Land of Darkness!"

"Please," the Heart replied, "just peace and quiet, not a revolution. All I need is one owner, not a big competition. Then, together, we can light up this land a little."

"Yeah, sure, great," she said, dragging along the Heart. "Be a good heart, don't cause trouble, and you will be fantastic."

The Heart appeared on the woman's television show.
It really was a revolution—more like tons of confusion.
In the studio, the telephones were ringing off the hook.
The excited audience surrounded the nervous Heart.

So badly did everyone want the new sensation that they began to tug and pull.

Feeling hurt, sad and used, the Heart ran out of the television studio. He wanted to escape from the Land of Darkness. People really were "heartless."

   Sitting in a park, feeling hopeless, the Heart saw a
little girl who was playing.   The child smiled a smile
that moved the Heart.

   "Would you let me in there?" the Heart finally said,
pointing to her chest. The child looked confused. "Who
are you?" she asked.

"I am the desire to cry, to laugh, to play," explained the Heart. "I like to help people love one another. Didn't you see me on television?"

"I don't like to watch television," said the Child. "But I think I already have you in my chest."

"Do you really?" wondered the Heart.

"I think so," replied the Child. "But I haven't been around that long."

"Then why is this land always so dark?" asked the Heart.

"It's not that dark to me," said the Child, smiling. Stunned, the Heart took another look around. She was right!

"If you want to come inside," offered the Child, "jump in."

The Heart went in. It was a perfect combination: A child plus a heart equals pure love.

The Child and her new heart traveled around the Land of Darkness. One by one, they gathered up as many children as they could.

Soon, the Land of Darkness became brighter. The trees turned green and the sky blue.

United, the children taught the adults, or reminded those who had forgotten, that the Land of Darkness could become the Land of Light—if every person had a heart.

Let your own heart speak.

Give it a chance to play,

create and lighten up

the world around you.

FIVE WAYS THAT YOU CAN LET YOUR HEART SPEAK

- Don't pick fights. Find peaceful solutions to problems.

- Respect other people's opinions and points of view; don't ignore what they are saying. It is OK to disagree, but try to understand how and why they feel the way they do.

 - If it is possible to help out a friend, then do so.

- Don't hide from all problems by saying "There's nothing I can do." Be creative. Always seek out a positive answer.

- Don't become isolated. Stay informed, participate as much as you can, and work together.

Know of other ways to let your heart speak? E-mail at semfront@superlink.net and tell us what you are doing in your schools and communities to promote tolerance and compassion.

We are supporters of UNICEF

Created by the United Nations General Assembly in 1946 to help children after World War II in Europe, UNICEF helps children get the care and stimulation they need in the early years of life and encourages families to educate girls as well as boys. It strives to reduce childhood death and illness and to protect children in the midst of war and natural disaster. UNICEF supports young people, wherever they are, in making informed decisions about their own lives, and strives to build a world in which all children live in dignity and security.

For more information about UNICEF, visit: www.unicef.org

For more information about the United Nations General Assembly, visit: www.un.org

Above information is reprinted by permission from UNICEF